ELLA

Diaries

TOP SECRET!

Thanks to the sensational soccer stars from
Gold Street Clifton Hill PS and Boroondara Park
PS—and the always amazing Mo Johnson!—M.C.

Meredith Costain

For our soccer stars Lauren,
Jade, Zoe and all of the
Rooettes and Sapphires.—D.M.

Danielle McDonald

First American Edition 2021
Kane Miller, A Division of EDC Publishing

Text copyright © Meredith Costain, 2018
Illustrations copyright © Danielle McDonald, 2018

First published by Scholastic Australia, an imprint of Scholastic Australia Pty Limited.
This edition published under license from Scholastic Australia Pty Limited.

Library of Congress Control Number: 2020949894

Printed and bound in the United States of America

1 2 3 4 5 6 7 8 9 10

ISBN: 978-1-68464-304-2

ELLA Diaries

GOAL POWER

Kane Miller
A DIVISION OF EDC PUBLISHING

Monday, after school

Dear Diary,

Guess what? Amethyst is organizing a Lunchtime Soccer Club. And she's asked Zoe and me to be in it!

Amethyst is in our class. She is really, really, REALLY excellent at soccer. She used to play on the girls' soccer

Soccer STAR

team at her last school, before she came to ours. And she says her team won gazillions of games, all the time!

We don't have a girls' soccer team at our school because most of the seriously sporty girls play on the school basketball team. But a

♥ LUNCHTIME ♥

SOCCER CLUB

sounds like so much fun! And I already know a tiny bit about soccer because we sometimes play it in PE.

Plus my little sister, Olivia, plays on a team with her BFF, Matilda, so I've watched some of their games. (Even though her team is only a BABY TEAM for BABIES.)

olivia
Matilda
BABY soccer

Ammy (which is short for Amethyst and MUCH easier to spell) is totally CRAZY about soccer!

So crazy that she had her birthday party last week at this place called Soccer Land, where all the staff wear matching soccer outfits. You get to eat snacks shaped like sweet little soccer balls and watch videos with names like *The 20 Best Soccer Goals of All Time* on a giant TV screen and do soccer things like ball kicking and running up and down a lot.

Soccer-ball CUPCAKES

LOLLIPOPS

DRINKS

YUM

I couldn't go to Ammy's party because I had an exTREMEly scratchy throat that day and Mom thought I might have been getting a ~~contagers~~ contagious disease, which means everyone else's throats might get scratchy too. So I stayed home and watched a lovely nature documentary, all about wolverines, quietly on the couch instead.

MY SickBED

But Zoe went. And now she is crazy, crazy, crazy about soccer as well! She and Ammy spend all day talking about soccer stuff with weird names like:

corners

fouls

and dribbling

(which last time I checked is something that BABIES do. Bleuchhh).

But the rest of it
sounds fabulous.
Especially the ball
kicking and running
up and down a lot.

And guess what? We're going to start
our ♥ LUNCHTIME SOCCER CLUB
tomorrow.

Wish me luck, Diary!

Yours,
Ella
XOXO

Monday, ten minutes later

Zoe just called to say that Ammy has decided to put together a Lunchtime Soccer Club Committee! (LSCC for short.)

The LSCC will get to do extremely serious and important stuff like deciding all the soccer club rules, and who's allowed to ~~acksh~~ actually be in the club.

This is who's going to be on the committee.

AMMY

COMMITTEE
MEMBER
NUMBER ①

ZOE

COMMITTEE
MEMBER
NUMBER ②

ME

COMMITTEE
MEMBER
NUMBER ③

YES! I ♥ being on committees!

And there is going to be an Emergency
Meeting of the LSCC in ten minutes.

We usually have Emergency Meetings right

here, in my bedroom. I have to be careful
to KEEP OUT any annoying little brothers
or sisters (this means YOU, Olivia) in
case they snoop on our meeting then blab
important information to their best friends
(who then blab it to THEIR best friends,
until the WHOLE WILD
WORLD knows our
plans).

MY
ROOM

KEEP
OUT

But *this* time it won't be a problem because the Emergency Meeting is going to be at Ammy's house* instead.

* Ammy's house is *exactly* halfway between Zoe's house and my house.

I know this because I measured it once
with an exTREMEly long piece of string
for a math project at school.

Ball of String

Got to go, Diary. Or else there won't be
time for our meeting before Mom says I
have to be home for dinner.

Talk soon!
E

Monday night, in bed

Dearest Diary,

We had our ELSCCM (Emergency Lunchtime Soccer Club Committee Meeting) in Ammy's bedroom. And it was amazing! And exciting! And fantastically fabulous!*

* The meeting, not Ammy's bedroom. Although that is amazingly amazing as well.

Ammy's bedroom has gazillions of soccer things in it. Like a light shaped like a soccer ball hanging from the ceiling and a soccer-themed bedspread and curtains.

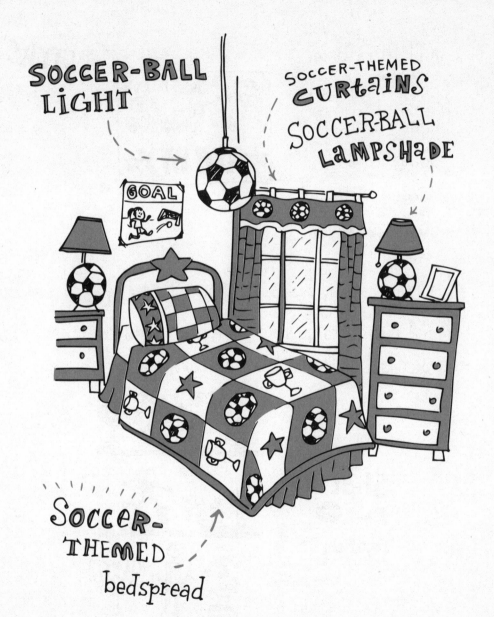

SOCCER-BALL LIGHT

SOCCER-THEMED CURTAINS

SOCCER-BALL LAMPSHADE

GOAL

SOCCER-THEMED bedspread

And there are posters of girls running about doing snazzy soccer kicks all over the walls.

POSTERS

★AMMY★

And the shelves are full of all the trophies and cups Ammy has won for being excellently excellent at soccer.

Shelves FULL OF TROPHIES

And guess what's on her bookshelf?

Books, all about soccer! And Ammy said Zoe
and I could borrow them anytime we want!
So Zoe took one. And I took six. ☺☺☺

After some snacks** and general chitchat about school, we started our ELSCCM.

** I was hoping these might be those sweet little soccer-ball-shaped ones like everyone (except me ☹) had at ~~Socker~~ Soccer Land, but they were just normal, standard, boring, regular, everyday snacks like we have at home.

Fruit

Fruit Juice

COOKIES

Muffins

I was the "official note taker" because I have the neatest handwriting. (We had a vote.) Here are the notes I made about our meeting:

① The Lunchtime Soccer Club will be ~~strickly~~ strictly Girls Only.

NO BOYS ALLOWED

② Anyone who wants to can be in our club, as long as they're in { GRADE 5 }.
Unless they're BOYS. (See point Number ①.)

3 Ammy will teach everyone all the different soccer skills and explain all about The Rules of Soccer (and provide easy-to-follow diagrams in different colored markers to help explain them) if they don't already know how to play.

BEND GOAL

KICK

Diagrams

(They probably don't know how to play because apart from Ammy I'm pretty sure everyone else has only ever played soccer a few times, when we did it for PE.

And most of that was spent trying not to kick other people's legs when we were ~~acksherly~~ actually aiming for the ball. Oh, and running up and down a lot.)***

*** This **PART** wasn't actually in the **meeTing**. I just added it in **LaTeR**.

④ Once everyone knows how to play we will appoint two captains who will each get to choose players for their team.

CAPTAIN ①   CAPTAIN ②

I hope to be one of these!

This day will be known (both now and forevermore) as **TEAM-PICKING DAY,** or TPD for short.

5 The two teams will play soccer games against each other at lunchtimes.

6 Lunchtime Soccer Club will be fun, fun, fun at all times!

Zoe, Ammy and I made a poster about our club to stick up on the big bulletin board in the Grade 5 area in the morning.

ATTENTION! GRADE FiVE STUDENTS!!

★ GiRLS ONLY ★

WARNING.
READ THIS
PART HERE.

DO YOU LIKE:
1. Kicking balls?
2. Running around a LOT?
3. Being part of a TEAM?
4. Having FUN, FUN, FUN?

Then come to the SCHOOL FIELD at lunchtime and JOIN our

LUNCHTiME SOCCER CLUB

We also made stylish badges with LSCC on them, so that everyone would know that we were important, official members of the LUNCHTIME **SOCCER CLUB** COMMITTEE.

Then we all just sat there, dreamily, on Ammy's soccer-themed bed for a bit, looking at each other with shiny eyes, thinking about how much fun tomorrow was going to be.

And then Ammy's eyes got even shinier, almost as shiny as the light in her soccer-ball lamp, and she said, "I can't wait until tomorrow. I want to get started RIGHT NOW."

Then she started to tell us about a
complicated soccer thing called the
offside rule.

She was just using her pencil
case and pencil sharpener
and colored markers to show
what being offside ~~acksh~~
actually means when my
brain started to explode (and
so did Zoe's, even though
she already knows
heaps more about
soccer than me
because of going
to Soccer Land).

pencil case

ME

ZOE

EXPLODING BRAINS!!!

So we both just said, "Ooooo, look, is that the time?"

and, "Thank you very much for a lovely Emergency Meeting,"

and, "We'll see you at school tomorrow."

And then we ran home (in opposite directions) before Ammy could think of any more complicated rules to explain to us.

I told Mom and Dad and Olivia and Max all about the Lunchtime Soccer Club while we were having dinner. (Which was Chicken à la King, in case you were wondering. With carrots and peas.

BLEUCHHH!

And boiled rice with lumpy bits in it.

<u>DOUBLE</u> bleuchhh.)

Peas

Carrots

CHICKeN à La KiNG

BOILED RICE

I thought Olivia would be super interested
to hear all about it (on account of the
fact that she plays soccer too, even if it's
with a bunch of BABIES) and say nice,
supportive, sisterly things like,

"Wow, Ella, that's so exciting!"

and, "We'll be able to discuss
strategies and practice
interesting soccer moves
together on the weekend and
after school."

Olivia

But guess what? She didn't.

She just went on
secretly playing this
game with Max to see
who could balance the
most peas on their nose

before Mom noticed and made them pick up
all the ones that fell off their noses and
rolled onto the table and onto the floor and
then got all squished under everybody's feet
or licked by Bob.

Eww. Squished peas.
with dog lick on
them. ☹

But Dad was. (Super interested, I mean.)

He got all excited and told us all about the soccer games he used to play when he was in Grade 5 (about 900 years ago during the ice age).

Sad
DAD

And then he started explaining all about
what the offside rule is too. Only he used
salt and pepper shakers and the ketchup
bottle and knives and forks instead of
pencil cases and markers.

I had to stop him halfway through because I
don't think it is very healthy for my brain
to explode TWICE in one day.

After dinner, Dad made us all squish up together on the couch to watch a DVD of ancient soccer games from the olden days, called *The Greatest Soccer Players of All Time.*

The soccer players had names like Pelé. And Maradona. And Kaká. And every time someone scored a goal, all their teammates ran around the field like mad things with their shirts pulled up over their faces. And you could see their tummies and hairy chests.

Eww. I hope we don't have to do that when
we score a goal. 😐

Good night, Diary. I'd better get some sleep
now so I'm nice and fresh for our first
Lunchtime Soccer Club tomorrow!

Sweet dreams,
Ella xOxO

Tuesday, after school

Dear Diary,

Zoe and Ammy and I got to school really early so we could put our LSC poster up on the bulletin board in the Grade 5 area before everyone else arrived.

As soon as the lunchtime bell rang we quickly pinned our LSCC badges on. Then we ran over to the school field with a big bag of soccer balls Ammy borrowed from Ms. Astrellano, our PE teacher, and waited nervously by the fence for new club members to show up.

We waited . . .

and waited . . .

and waited . . .

until, finally . . .

The Good News

Lots of my friends from our class turned up! Like Cordelia. And Poppy and Daisy. And Chloe and Georgia. ☺☺☺

The Bad News

Some of my *non-friends* from our class also turned up. Like Precious Princess Peach Parker, the most annoying and smirky person in the history of annoying smirky people. And her two annoying sneery BFFs, Prinny and Jade. ☹☹☹

Precious PEACH PARKER

Jade

Prinny

NON-FRIENDS

The Better News

Some girls from the other Grade 5 class turned up too, like Aisha and Carly and

Tessa, plus heaps of Peach's gym friends.
And guess what?

Aisha and Carly play for a
soccer team on Saturday
mornings, called the Yarra
Rangers. Which means they
already know how to play. YES!

The Awful, Terrible, Rotten, Horrendously Horrible, Not-Good News

We were all just walking onto the field
so we could start doing some ball-kicking
practice when Peter and Raf ran
over. And they didn't look happy.

This is what happened next.

Peter and Raf (frowning): Hey!

Me (surprised): Hey, what?

Zoe (also surprised): Yeah. Hey, what?

Peter: What are all you GIRLS doing here?

Me (rolling my eyes): Picking daisies.

Zoe (also rolling her eyes): Yeah. So we can make daisy chains.

Raf (confused): Huh? But there aren't any—

Ammy (kicking her ball to Aisha): We're playing soccer. What does it look like we're doing?

Peter: But you can't.

Me: Says who?

Zoe: Yeah. Says who?

Raf: Says us. This is where the BOYS play.
Peter: Yeah, this field is strictly for boys only!

PETER   RaF

BOYS ONLY!

I was SHOCKED. And so were Zoe and Ammy.

Me: Since when?
Raf: Since forever.
Peter: Yeah. NO GIRLS ALLOWED.

SHOCKED!

Ammy   ME   ZOE

And then Peach came over and said, "Come on, let's go. Who wants to play in the same place as smelly boys anyway."

Peach said that. Peach NEVER stands up for me. Ever.

Then everyone else in our soccer club said, "Yeah. Let's get out of here."

So Ammy picked up her ball
and we all walked back off
the field and over to this
MUCH NICER part of the
school grounds.

It's on the other side of the
basketball courts,
where there are
lots of flowers and
trees and birds and
praying mantises
to look at and no
smelly boys to
worry about.

Then Ammy told us all how to play this
amazing game called Sharks and Minnows
they used to play at her last school. She
said it was a really excellent way to
practice our dribbling.*

* Guess what?!
Dribbling doesn't ~~acksh~~
actually mean that thing

X Baby DROOL!

that babies do, when they have long trails
of icky, disgusting drool coming out of their
mouths. (Eww.)

It's the word you use when you want to
describe how soccer players move the
ball up and down the field, giving it little

tapping taps this way and then that way
with their feet.

Peach and Carly got chosen to be the scary
sharks and stand in the middle of our
NICER playing area.

MINNOWS

SHARKS

Carly

Peach

All the rest of us were the meek little minnows. We had to dribble our balls all the way from one side to the other, then back again. And then the sharklike sharks had to try and get our balls off us and kick them safely away. And if they did, then we turned into sharks too! And had to go after other minnows!

We kept playing until all the balls had been kicked away by scheming sharks into the faraway distance and there was only one teensy tiny brave little minnow left.

And guess who it was?

ZOE

None of the sharks could get her ball away from her. Even the really excellent players like Ammy and Aisha.

She is what my dad would call a "demon dribbler." Who knew?

MINNOW ZOE

SHARK AISHA

It was aMAZing! And EXcellent! And fantastically fabulous fun! Even if I did trip over while I was doing a big dribble and got turned into a shark by Princess Peach almost ~~imederatly~~ ~~immeediatly~~ straightaway. ☹

I can't wait to do it all again tomorrow!

E

xx

Tuesday night, in bed

Dear Diary-doo,

I've just been reading all about the different types of soccer players there are in one of Ammy's excellent soccer books.

Here are the main ones.

TYPES OF SOCCER PLAYERS AND WHAT THEY DO

Type of player	Do I want to be one?	Why or why not
 **STRIKER** Kicks all the goals. They are the fastest at running and the best dribblers.	YES YES YES YES YES YES YES YES YES YES YES YES YES YES YES 100% to the power of a gazillion	Because kicking goals is fabulous fun and everyone screams "Yes!" and calls out your name and gives you a big hug or high-fives you when you do it.

DEFENDER Tries to stop the other team from scoring by running up and down in front of the goal a lot.	Not really	You don't get a chance to kick any goals because you're at the **wrong end** all the time. ☹
MIDFIELDER Passes the ball and runs up and down a lot.	Maybe	This one sounds a bit boring. And you have to do most of the work for none of the glory.
Sweeper Sweeps up all the trash that rude people drop after the game is over.✻	Definitely not	This one sounds **exTREMEly** boring. ✻Oops! I think this is the wrong kind of sweeper. ☺

GOALKEEPER

Stops the other team from getting any goals by reaching up high and grabbing the ball out of the air or kicking it away or taking a flying leap and diving on top of it.

Maybe. You get to wear a different outfit and you could make it very stylish and ~~yuneek~~ unique. You don't have to run very much which would be handy if you had a sore foot.

This one is very tricky. If you save a goal, people will cheer for you and love you. But what about if you miss the ball and everyone calls out BOOOOO? That would be extremely hurtful. And if your team was really, really good, all the main action would be at the other end and it would be B.O.R.I.N.G. spells boring.

As you can see, a striker is the best and most ~~glamerous~~ glamorous thing to be. I don't know why they bother with any of the other positions because who would even want to play them?

I want to be a striker SOOOO MUCH!!! I hope I get to be one when we stop doing dribbling practice and start playing real games with teams.

Ooooooooooo, look. There's a star shining right outside my window. It must be a sign!

I'm going to wish on it RIGHT NOW.

Star light
Star bright
Here's the wish
I wish tonight
Please please please please please please
please (to infinity)
Let me be a striker on the LSC team!

Yours 4 ever and ever,
Ella
XOXO

Wednesday morning, very, very early, in bed still

Dear Diary,

I just had the most aMAZing dream!

I was in a gigantic stadium full of cheering crowds, wearing an exceptionally stylish and sporty long-sleeved top with pink and mauve stripes (my most favorite colors) and sweet little rows of miniature pom-poms down the sleeves. And I was tapping and tapping a ball with my feet toward a teeny tiny goal thing about a gazillion billion miles away. And I was swerving and swaying and veering and tilting and zigging and zagging around scary sharks and meek minnows while the crowds roared and roared, like hungry lions.

And then I kicked the ball right through the middle of the net.

GOAL!

And the crowds jumped out of their seats and ran around with all the players (from BOTH teams) with their shirts pulled up over their faces.✳

✳ ~~Forch~~ Fortunately in my dream they were all wearing another shirt underneath their top one.

another SHIRT underneath!

It was the best
dream I have EVER
HAD IN MY WHOLE
LIFE!

Do you think it might
be another sign? You
know, about getting
chosen to be one of
the strikers?

Because that would be aMAZing. And
EXcellent. And fanTAStically FABulous.

CYA,
Ella

Wednesday, after school

Dear Diary,

We had another meeting of the LSC today. Only this time, we didn't even bother going over to the field. We just went straight to our own NICER place near the trees.

We did **DRIBBLING**

and different kinds of **TRAPPING**

ZOE

1a With our <u>FOOT</u> part **1b**

AMMY

2a With our <u>TOP LEG</u> part **2b**

and **PASSING**

PEACH

Prinny

And guess what? I was hopelessly hopeless at EVERYTHING.

Especially dribbling.

Nobody said anything, but I could tell they all thought I was hopelessly hopeless as well. Especially Aisha and Carly.

How am I going to be a striking striker if I can't even dribble? ☹☹☹

Ella

Thursday, after school

Dear Diary,

Today we made a goal using some jump ropes, sweaters, and schoolbags.

And then we all lined up in a long line and took turns to kick the ball into the goal area between the trees.

But guess what? I was hopelessly hopeless at goal shooting too. ☹

PLACES MY BALLS ENDED UP

Up the **TREE** on the **LEFT**

Attempt ①

Up the **TREE** on the **RIGHT**!

ATTEMPT ②

ATTEMPT 3, Smack bang in the middle of Aisha's lunch. Oops! She didn't look very happy about it.

I'm never going to be a striker now.

Thursday night, in bed (very late—so late everyone else is in bed too)

Dear Diary,

I am in desperate despair.

Ammy has decided we all know enough soccer skills now to start playing ~~acksh~~ actual games. So tomorrow is going to be TPD (Team-Picking Day).

And nobody is going to want to choose me. ☹

Everything is hopelessly hopeless.

Yours in (almost) utter desolation,
Ella
XOXO

Thursday night, ten minutes later

I've just had an aMAZingly excellent idea!

I'm going to get up out of my Bed of Despair and stealthily creep* down the hallway and into the family room so I can watch that ancient DVD that Dad showed us.

You know, the one with all the fabulously famous goal-scoring soccer players from the ice age. Like Pelé. And Kaká. And ~~Maradoona~~ Maradona.

Their names are all over **AMMY'S** bedroom.

Stealthily **CREEPING**

* This is so I don't wake anyone up. Especially Bob. If I wake up Bob he is going to want food ~~immeed~~ straightaway and then I will probably wake up everyone else in the house when I give it to him because he is a very *crunchy* eater. And then all my plans will be foiled.**

✳✳ Foiled means wrecked or dashed or nipped in the bud. It does NOT mean wrapping things up in that shiny stuff you use when you are keeping pies warm.

I might be able to get some top goal-scoring tips from the DVD!

Stay right here safely under my pillow, dearest Diary. I will be back soon.

E

xoxo

Thursday night, six minutes after that

I'm back.

And guess what?

Max has been playing store with the DVDs again. And they're all hopelessly mixed up in the wrong cases. It's going to take me 900 hours (at least) to find the soccer one.

NOOOOOOOOO!

I was just standing in the middle of the family room, about to die of desperate despair (again), when I heard this kind of scuttling, scuffing, shuffling sound, coming along the hallway.

THINGS I THOUGHT THE SCUTTLING, SCUFFING, SHUFFLING SOUND MIGHT BE:

① **GIGANTIC** Slobbering **RATS**!!

2 Gigantic slobbering cockroaches with twitchy feelers.

3 Gigantic aliens with scaly feet that had accidentally put the wrong coordinates into the GPS thingy on their alien spacecraft and landed in our house instead of on the Planet Zog.

ALIEN

OUR HOUSE

scaly FEET

4 The famous soccer players from the DVD who had all mysteriously turned into ZOMBIFIED ZOMBIES and were coming to turn all of us into zombies too.

So I quickly shined my flashlight down the hallway to see who it was.

And guess what?

It was only Dad. On his way to the bathroom. ☺☺☺

AAARGGHHH!!!

Phewwwww.

Good night, Diary.
Ella
XOXO

Friday, after school

Dearest Diary,

Today was . . . gulp . . . TPD.

Everyone stood around in our LSC area,
casually doing rainbows and keepy-ups while
they waited to see which team they were
going to be on.

(Except for Ammy and Zoe and me because we were busy being the official LSCC members, with official LSCC badges and stylish matching pens and clipboards.)

First of all we had a vote to see who the two team captains were going to be. Everyone (including Ammy and Zoe and me) had to write down the name of the person they thought would do the best job on a piece of paper.

And then Zoe and I collected all the papers.

Then we added up **all the votes**. And guess who won?

Wait for it . . .

Drumroll . . .

Me!

(Hehe. Only joking. ☺☺☺)

It was actually Ammy who got the most votes.

And the second biggest vote getter was . . .

When Ammy read Princess Peach's name out, Peach squealed a little squeal and said, "Who? Me?" in this really fake, silvery voice she always uses. And then she gave a short speech about how she promised to do her best to be a caring and responsible captain at all times.

BLeuchhh!

Zoe and I were SHOCKED that Peach got picked. Even though we already knew she'd won because we'd just done all the vote counting.

I am SHOCKED!

So am I.

ME

ZOE

who would have even **voted** for her?

And then it hit me.

It must have been Peach's gymnastics friends from the other Grade 5 class that have been coming to the LSC every day. Plus her two sneering sidekicks, Prinny and Jade.

Guess how many votes I got?

I am feeling just a teeny tiny bit distraught, Diary, because not one single, solitary person out of the WHOLE LSC voted for me to be a team captain. Not even Zoe, and she's supposed to be my BFF. She voted for Ammy instead.✲ ☹

✲ I know this because I could tell which bit of paper was hers when we were counting up the votes. She always adds curls to the letter "A."

Next it was time for the team picking.

We all stood in a long line in front of the goalpost trees. Then Ammy and Peach took turns to choose which players they wanted on their team, until there was nobody left.

And guess who Ammy picked first?

HINT: Her name rhymes with snowy.

ZOE

And then it was Peach's turn. And guess who *she* picked first?

If you said Prinny or Jade then you are

WRONG! **WRONG!** WRONG!

Peach picked Aisha! And then Carly next.

AiSHa!
CaRLy!

Hehehe. I don't think Prinny and Jade were very happy about *that.* ☺

I was really, really, REALLY nervous that no one would pick me for their team, on account of being hopelessly hopeless at dribbling and trapping and goal kicking.

But guess what?

Ammy picked me next after Zoe. So I was safe!

When the two teams were finally picked we each did a big

GROUP HUG!

And then Peach gave another (slightly longer) speech about "pulling together" and the importance of TEAM SPIRIT.

And then she reminded everyone that her team would have to play EXTRA hard because it only had nine players on it which wasn't really fair because ours had ten.✳

* The Rules of Soccer say you are ~~acksh~~ actually supposed to have eleven players on a team, but Ammy says it doesn't even matter because LSC isn't  about winning—it's all about having fun, fun, fun at all times. YES!

I have to go now, Diary. Ammy and Zoe are coming over in exactly FIVE MINUTES for some extra soccer practice in the park, and I need to get my ~~skates~~ soccer shoes on!

Talk later!
E

Saturday night, after dinner

Dear Diary,

Ammy and Zoe came over for another Emergency Lunchtime Soccer Club Committee Meeting today so we could discuss **important** soccer strategies.

This time we had the meeting in my room.

MY ROOM!

There were Good and Bad Things about this.

Good Thing

It wouldn't take very long* for me to run home if Ammy started trying to explain any more complicated rules to us. Like a soccer corner kick. Or where your feet have to be during a soccer throw-in.

* ExACTly 0.00 seconds

ExACTLY
0.00 seconds

Bad Thing

Olivia threatened to throw one of her big tantrums if I didn't let her come to the meeting too. And Mom said I HAD TO. And then Max said he wanted to come too. So I had to let *him* in as well. (And also Bob.)

Here are some of the important soccer strategies we discussed in our meeting:

① What we are going to wear while we are playing.

Sequined NECK TRIM

LaYEReD RUffLED SLEEVES

TWO-TONE PiNK stripes

9

Sequined NUMBER ON BACK

PINK glitter shoes

2 Which position everyone will play.

FORWARDS

MIDFIELDERS

DEFENDERS

GOALKEEPER

3 And, most importantly of all, what our team will be called.

Here are some of the names we came up with:

Name	Whose idea?	Marks out of 10	Comments
AMMY'S AMIGOS	Ammy	4	People might think there were only three of us on the team.
AMMY'S **Amoebas**	Olivia	2	This one is just silly. ~~Ameobas~~ Amoebas don't even have any arms or legs (or heads or lungs or guts) so how can they play soccer? Plus it's too hard to spell.

AMMY'S PRAMMIES	Max	0	This one is even sillier.
AMMY'S Amphibians	Ella	6	This one would be hard to call out in a sports cheer.
AMMY'S AMBUSHERS	Zoe	8	The best one so far.
AMMY'S AMAZONS	Ella	10	YES! This one is PERFECT! And AMAZING! And FANTASTICALLY FABULOUS!!!

And guess which name we chose? ☺

♥

♥ MiNE! ♥

So now we're called Ammy's Amazons. I
hope the rest of the team likes it.

I can't wait to find out what Peach calls her
team!

PEACH'S PetaLS
Peach's PLUMS
Peach's pythons
PEACH'S pearLS
Peach's Pirates
PeACH'S Peacocks

Love,
Ella
X

PS I forgot to tell you some Very Sad News about our meeting.

Ammy doesn't think I've got the right kind of feet to be a striker.

WRONG KIND of **FEET!**

But she thinks I'll make an excellent defender instead.

And so does Zoe.

I'm trying really, really hard not to be too disappointed, Diary. At least I'm not goalkeeper. That would be REALLY BORING.

"SOB"

E

Sunday night, after dinner

Dear Diary,

Ammy and Zoe and I and some other members of our team—like Tessa and Marina from the other Grade 5 class—all met in the park today to do some extra soccer practice.

And guess what? They all LOVE, LOVE, LOVE the name for our team I thought up. ☺

And (most of) the designs I casually threw together for our uniforms. Except for this one. Which is just WEIRD. Anyone with even a tiny brain could see how inCREDibly classy and chic and stylishly stylish it is. ☹

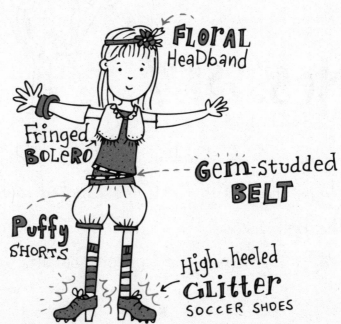

FLORAL HeaDband

Fringed BoLeRo

Gem-studded BELT

Puffy SHORTS

High-heeled GLitter SOCCER SHOES

Anyway, the type of soccer practicing we did today was all about how to be good at defending.

This was PERFECT for me! I'm going to be the best defender in the history of defenders!

Yesssss!

We all had to stand in two lines. And then a player from the first line started dribbling the ball across the middle part toward the players waiting in a line on the other side.

When they were almost halfway across, Ammy called out "Go!" And then a player from the second line had to race over to the first player and try to get the ball off them! Without using their hands! Or tripping them! Or pushing them over!

It was SOOOO EXCITING!

LINE 1

Dribbler

LINE 2

BALL

MIDDLE PART

DEFENDER

And then suddenly it was My turn!

Tessa was the dribbler and I was the defender.

Everything started off really well! I waited patiently in my spot on the second line for Ammy to call out "Go!" to me. And then as soon as she said it, I raced over to where Tessa was giving the ball little tapping taps with her foot.

GO!

ME

Zoe called out GO, ELLA!!

And so did all the rest of the players!
(Except for Tessa who was a bit busy
doing the dribbling.)

And then I swung my leg back and did a
gigantic defending kicky kick.

Gigantic
Defending
Kicky
Kick

~~unforch~~ Unfortunately, my foot part kicked
Tessa on the leg part instead of the ball.

And Tessa called out,

And everyone else called out, "FOUL!"

Then Ammy asked Zoe to be the person who called out "GO!" instead of her so she could give me some special individualized defending lessons. We went to another part of the park, far, far away from the other players and their leg parts.

which is just as well because tomorrow we are playing our first real game of lunchtime soccer FOR REAL.

I can't wait!

CU LatR, Diary,
Ella

PS I found out the name of Peach's soccer team!!!

Chloe overheard Prinny and Jade and their other gymnastics friends talking about it when

chloe

they were all doing gym class at Twisters yesterday morning. Then Chloe told Georgia, and Georgia told Poppy, and Poppy told Daisy, and Daisy told Zoe, and Zoe told me.

And guess what it is?

Peach's Piranhas

Sunday night, in bed

Dear Diary,

Here is a soccer chant I just wrote for our first game against Peach's Piranhas.
I hope everyone likes it.

We are the Amazons
We're proud and we're strong
We're soccer-playing sisters
And we always get along

We are the Amazons
We're strong and we're proud
We're kickers and we're trickers and
We're very, very LOUD!

A — M — A — Z — O — N — S spells . . .

AMAZONS

And then at the end we can all
do cartwheels across the field.

It's going to be aMAZing!

Bye,

E

Monday, after school

Dear Diary,

We played our first LSC game.

And guess what happened?

WARNING:

I did the ~~worserest~~ worst, most shocking, horrible, terrible thing anyone can ever, ever do in the history of shocking, horrible, terrible things you can do when you're playing soccer.

It's even worse than kicking someone in the leg part when you're practicing defending.

I kicked an OWN GOAL.* And it wasn't even my fault! (OK, maybe a bit.)

* An own goal is another one of those really, really, really (to the power of a gazillion) complicated things that makes your head explode when someone tries to explain it to you. So it's probably best to just TRUST ME when I say it's a really, really bad and extremely embarrassing thing to do.

Here's what happened.

The score was:

| Ammy's AMAZONS | 1 |
| Peach's PiRanHAS | 1 |

And it was nearly the end of lunchtime!

So the team that scored the next goal would be

WINNERS
ARE
GRiNNERS!!

Peach's Piranhas were all playing really, really ~~sharkerously~~ piranha-ously and the ball kept coming down to my end. Which meant that the other defenders and I had to do lots of defending and stop the ball and kick it back up to the other end before someone kicked it into our goal.

And everyone was running up and down really, really fast and calling out things like:

and

and it got REALLY CONFUSING.

And then, all of a sudden, the ball was flying through the air, straight at me. So I called out:

And then . . . .

Da da da....

Dummm.

I jumped up really high and
caught it. With my hands.
Just like you do when
you're playing basketball.

Except you're not allowed to touch the ball
with your hands when you're playing soccer.
It is banned and
barred and ~~strickly~~
strictly forbidden
AT ALL TIMES.
(Unless you are
the goalkeeper.
Which I wasn't. ☹)

FORBIDDEN
AT ALL TIMES!!

So then the other player got a free kick. And guess who it was?

Peach Parker.

And then all of a sudden Prinny had the ball, and she was passing it to Jade.

And then Jade passed it back to Peach. And then Peach did a big kick, straight toward the goal.

And then . . . KAZOW! . . . I started
running toward it so I could do one of
those excellent trapping things Ammy
showed us how to do, and save the day like
Kaká always did!

And everyone was cheering and calling out,

Go, ELLA!

Go, ELLA!

Go, Ella!

And I got closer

and closer

and closer

and then right at the very last second, when
I was just about to trap the ball with my
foot part, I tripped.

And fell over.

And the ball hit my foot.

And then rolled off it.

Right into the middle of our goal.

And we lost the game.

NOOOOOOOO!

I'm too upset right now to write about what happened after that. Maybe I could manage a few lines later, Diary, if I haven't died of COMPLETE AND UTTER DESOLATION by then.

1 2 3 4 5 6 7 8 9 10
                                    X

MILD   DESPAIR   MAJOR   DESPERATE   UTTER
DESPAIR   DESPAIR   DESPAIR   DESOLATION!

Yours in sadness,
Ella
XOXO ☹

Monday night, in bed

Dear Diary,

OK, I think I'm ready to write about what happened now.

Here it comes.

WARNING: EXTRA EXTRA STRONG TISSUE ALERT

(The really thick kind you use when you have a really snotty cold and you don't want it to break because then the snotty snot will go all over your hand. Eww.)

Ammy came up to me in the Grade 5 area when we were getting our bags ready to go home. She said she'd been having a quick chat about all our soccer field positions with Zoe and Tessa.

And then she asked me if I'd like to stop being a defender for a while and have a little try at being goalkeeper instead.

NOOOOOOOO!

My heart is irretrievably* broken.
Forever. (And ever.)

BROKEN
HEART

* "Irretrievably" is a special word
you use to describe what happens when
you can never fix something or get it
back again. Like when you are throwing a
very expensive squeaky ball for your dog
(let's call him Bob) and it accidentally rolls
down a grassy slope and into a ~~deep, dark,
bottomless~~ pit that a ~~plumming~~ plumbing
lady is digging for a new pipe because the
old one burst and gigantic plumes of water
went everywhere including all over your
exceptionally stylish new shoes.

And you don't want
to crawl down into
the pit to get
it because it is
extremely muddy and icky
down there (and there may
also be slimy slugs. Eww).

ME

BOB

BOB'S Expensive SQUEAKY BALL

DEEP DARK BOTTOMLESS PIT

← Slimy SLUGS

LSC is supposed to be fun, fun, fun at all times.

But it's not. ☹

Why, Diary? Why?

Tuesday, before dinner

Dearest Diary,

Today was my first day of being goalkeeper.

It started off really, really excellently. All the running up and down and kicking and passing and trapping and goal scoring action, action, action was up at the other end this time. So I had plenty of time to enjoy one of my second-most favorite things—nature.

I was just rescuing this sweet little praying mantis that had wandered into the back of our goal net and gotten itself all tangled up and thinking up words for a new poem called "The Dangly Tangly Praying Mantis" when . . .

Da da da . . .

Dummm.

All of a sudden there was a huge rush of
stampeding feet, and all the players from
BOTH teams came charging toward me like
rampaging minotaurs.*

Rampaging Minotaurs

* I know all about minotaurs because I am
doing a project on these for our unit on
Ancient Myths of Greece and Rome at school
at the moment.

So I quickly put the praying mantis in a safe place behind one of the goal trees and stood there, proud and strong, like a true goalkeeper, ready to stop any goals that came my way.

Praying Mantis

Prinny had the ball. She tapped it to Jade and then Jade passed it to Carly and Carly backheeled it to Peach.

And then Peach slammed the ball toward the right-hand corner of the goal area. Like this:

WHAM!

And guess what happened next?

You won't be able to and even if you can you'll probably get the wrong answer so I'll just tell you.

I did a big diving dive! And I caught the
ball, just as it came flying into the corner
of the goal area off Peach's foot! And
this time it didn't matter that my hands
touched it because goalkeepers are
allowed to. YESSSSSSS!

And everyone
on my team
screamed:

GOOD SAVE!

I stood there for a few moments in the
sunny sunshine holding the ball, feeling
proud and strong and Amazonish.

And then everyone on my team screamed again:

"ELL-AAAA! THROW THE BALL! NOW!"

I looked and looked and LOOKED for someone to throw the ball to. But Peach's Piranhas were everywhere.

The Amazons were trapped!

And then suddenly Zoe did a tricky twisty move around the back of Prinny, right into a lovely big empty patch of flowery grass.

So I threw the ball to her.

~~unforch~~ Unfortunately it went a bit high and she had to trap it with her chest part instead of her foot part. Ouch. ☹

ZOE

As soon as the ball hit the ground again, Zoe kicked it over to Ammy, who passed it to Marina, and everyone ran off back down

to the other end of the field to the other
goal part again.

It was all so **Exciting!**

And **AMAZING!**

AND fantastically **FABULOUS!**

Maybe being the goalkeeper
isn't so ~~booring~~ boring after all!

Love,
Ella

Wednesday, after school

Dearest, darlingest Diary,

I CANNOT WAIT to tell you what happened at LSC today!

I did another save! And it was even more spectacularly spectacular than the one I did yesterday!

Even MORE SPECTACULAR!

This time it was Aisha and Carly doing all
the main dribbling. And our defenders couldn't
stop them. They just kept tapping and
passing and backheeling to each other over
and over again. And then Aisha did a really
big kicky kick, right in front of the goal part.

And it was coming straight at me!

And guess what? Instead of catching it, I
did a big leaping leap into the
air. Just like I do when I'm
doing a pas de chat*
at ballet class.

Pas de chat

* Pas de chat is French for "step of the cat." Isn't that sweet?

Pas de chat

And then I gracefully stuck my arm up in the air (also like how I do in ballet, only much faster) and flicked the ball up over the top of the goal part and out of danger.

And everyone screamed, "GOOD SAVE!" again. Only much louder this time!

And guess who saw me do it? Ms. Astrellano, our PE teacher, who just happened to be walking past on her way to the teachers' parking lot right at that very minute. She called out "Good save!" as well.

Ms. Astrellano

Good Save!

It was

EXCELLENT!

And

Magnificent!

And

Splendily
SPLENDID!

I want to be goalkeeper forever and ever and ever!

Yours,
Ella
X

PS (One week later)

Guess what? I am now the official goalkeeper for Ammy's Amazons at Lunchtime Soccer Club! And I'm getting better and better at diving and trapping and throwing back out every day.

OFFICIAL
GOALKEEPER

NAME: ELLA
TEAM: Ammy's
AMAZONS

And guess what else?

Ms. Astrellano came back AGAIN to watch us play.

And she said we were so excellent she's going to pick the best players for a Girls' School Soccer Team (GSST), just like the boys have! (Only with girls instead of boys on it.)

GSST

And she said we can do our practice on the main field ANYTIME we want.

I hope she picks me to be goalkeeper! I'm going to practice really, really hard and watch Dad's ancient old soccer DVDs and read all of Ammy's soccer books every chance I get!

Love,
Ella

BOOKS AND DVDs

PPS (Two weeks later)

Guess what? Ms. Astrellano picked the players for the GSST today.

And guess who's on it?

We'll always still be Amazons though. ☺

We are the Amazons
We're proud and we're strong
We're soccer-playing sisters
And we always get along
We are the Amazons
We're strong and we're proud
We're kickers and we're trickers and
We're very, very LOUD!
A — M — A — Z — O — N — S spells . . .

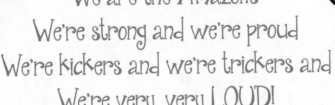

AMAZONS!

Diaries

Read more brilliant diaries!